Kicks

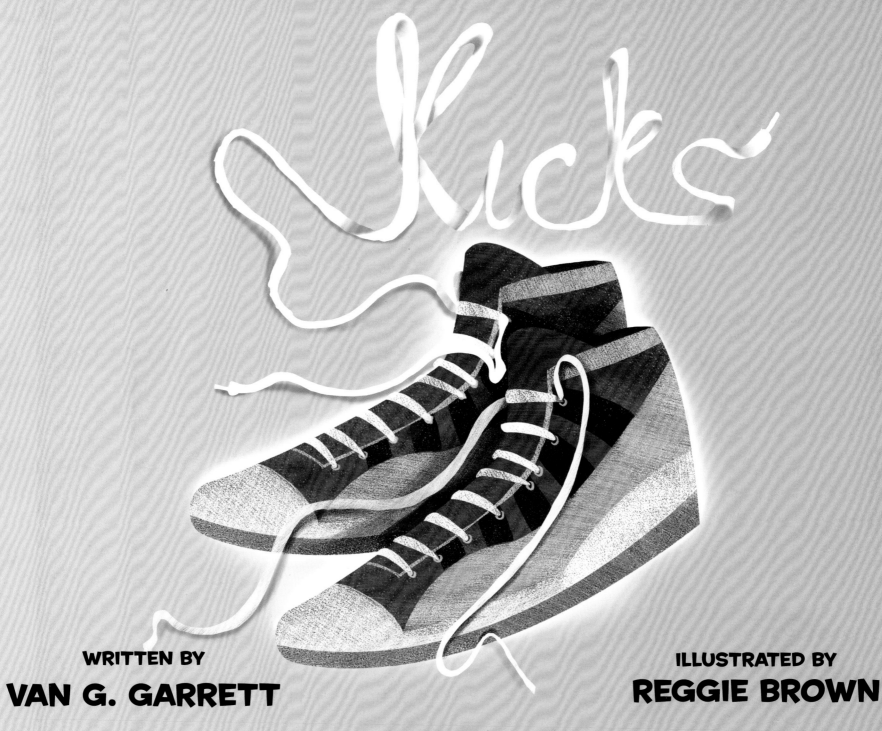

WRITTEN BY
VAN G. GARRETT

ILLUSTRATED BY
REGGIE BROWN

VERSIFY
An Imprint of HarperCollins*Publishers*
Boston   New York

Kicks
Text copyright © 2022 by Van G. Garrett
Illustrations copyright © 2022 by Reggie Brown

The Library of Congress Cataloging-in-Publication Data is on file.
ISBN: 978-0-358-11810-7

The illustrations in this book were created digitally.
The text type was set in Amasis MT.
The display type was set in House-a-Rama.

Manufactured in Italy
RTLO 10 9 8 7 6 5 4 3 2 1
4500842992

First edition

You can't pick **KICKS**
the way you pick sticks,
or stones, or dinosaur bones.

New kicks should be legit.
Not busted, hard, or old.

Magic for your soles
and soul.

A feeling of **WOW**—the way fireworks work clouds.

Like pizza with the right ingredients:
CRISPY. ASTOUNDING.

Smooth like hot-buttered
garlic bread.

soles

LEATHER

COLORS

SHOEMART

Get Them
AIR MAX 3
ENERGIZED
HERE!!!

OPEN

LINE
STARTS
HERE

You can't wait to try them on.
Eyes alert,
that fresh scent of a new release,
live out of the box,

soon to be paired with multicolored
or icy-white ankle or tube socks.

A confident, snug feeling
making your insides smile.

NEW KICKS feel like
treats for your feet.
Cereal in your biggest bowl.

Leather not creased, tight laces,
honeycomb bottoms sweet on the floor.
Allowing you to **ZOOM** like a racecar.

She has hers.
He has his.

Big cats, *three stripes*, *checks*.
Letters, numbers, waves of color
smooth under your fingertips.

Heat for your feet,
gloves for your toes.
So many styles and forms.
Detailed art:
swirls, loops, and patterns.

Legendary.
Like LeBron and Jordan.

Danica, Serena, and Simone.

Relax your shoulders,
do your too-cool walk,
enjoying leather, suede, or canvas
on a magic carpet ride.

Tongues upright as soldiers.
Fat strings pulled and tied.

The perfect look.
The perfect feel
for your everyday wardrobe,

or basketball games,

skateboarding,
and hopscotching.

Moonwalking.

Tiptoeing.
Soft-shoeing.

Hanging out with your family
and friends at cookouts,
movies, school, and
everywhere else you can imagine.

Even on rainy days,
you sparkle
in colorways
under an umbrella.

Soaking up experiences as you float,
like ice cream in Vanilla Coke.

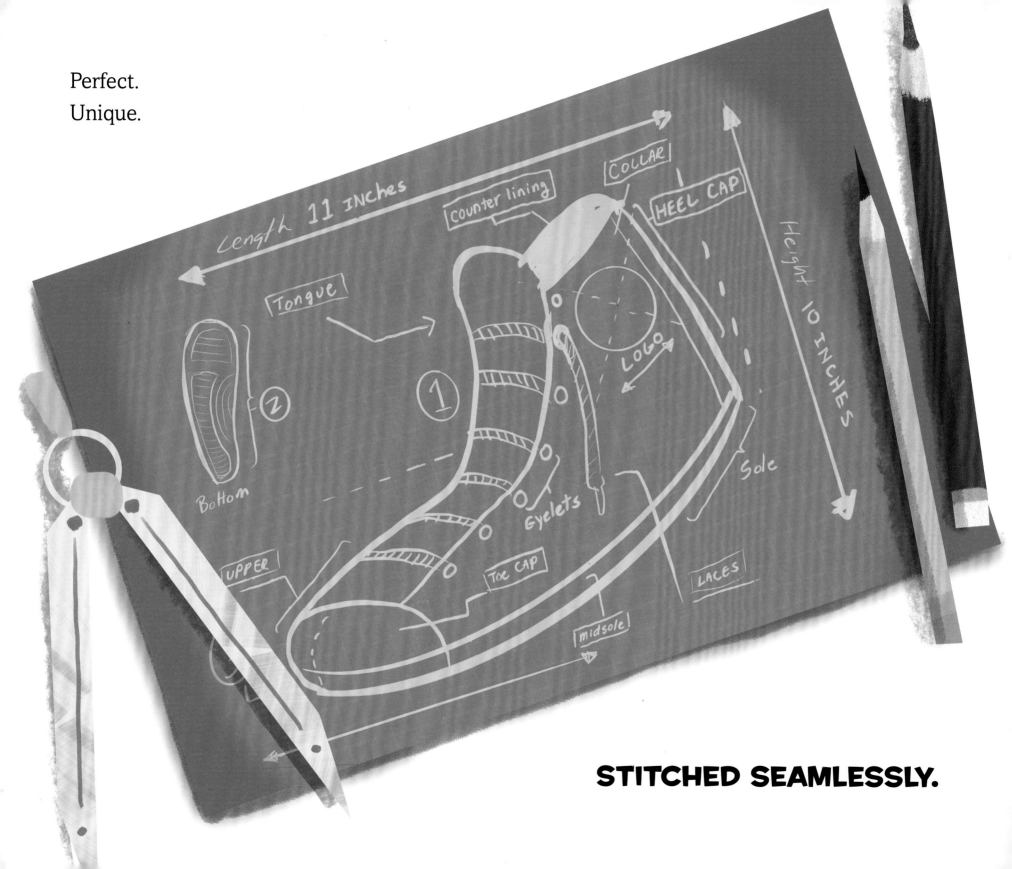

Kicks help you shine
like the brightness of sunrays
and new money, even when you have
a shoestring-tight allowance.

Giving you hope for days
when you can **LEAP**,

SOAR,

Sky-touching.
Feet off the ground,
head lifted high with a lion's pride.
Dreaming and feeling

EXCEPTIONAL.